D0654247

so, the sole survivor of the crash was swept away, barely conscious, by the powerful currents.

Survival time in the icy waters of the Baltic Sea is very short, but the boy was fortunate. The prevailing currents and rolling waves pitched him onto a sandy beach in Gotland, a large island off the coast of Sweden, just south of Stockholm. There he lay, shivering and barely breathing, for nearly two days.

*   *   *   *   *   *   *   *   *   *   *

Suffering from hypothermia and close to death, the boy was found by a pack of grey wolves scavenging for shellfish and other tasty morsels washed up by the tide. To the hungry animals, this helpless creature seemed to offer a hearty meal. However, they were prevented from closing in for the kill by their pack leader, an elderly and grizzled she-wolf called Lupe.

Lupe was fascinated by the boy's appearance. He

had shaggy brown hair that flashed grey in the sunshine, piercing amber-coloured eyes and a long, pointed face. He also had two unusually large canine teeth either side of his mouth, which he exposed with each laboured breath. His uncanny resemblance to a wolf endeared him to her. No longer able to breed, but still possessing powerful maternal instincts, Lupe saw in this helpless, wolf-like boy the possibility of bringing up one final cub.

The teenager lived with the wolves for over two years. During that time, he grew to trust and respect them and in return they accepted him as one of their own. In another wolf pack, he would have been expected to challenge for alpha status along with the other young males, but not here. The position of dominant wolf and pack leader was clearly occupied by Lupe.

Of course, there were many downsides to the boy's new life. Living rough in all weathers was very harsh, though the island's strangely temperate climate made this just about bearable. Consuming raw meat was his greatest hardship, but he forced himself to eat alongside his wolf family and supplemented his diet with wild fruit and berries that were plentiful in the woods. Above all, he was mindful that his stay with the pack depended on him behaving like a real wolf; he learnt their ways of dominance and submission, loyalty and cooperation, patience ... and, above all, cunning. Running on all fours, howling and barking, snuggling up to the others for warmth on the cold, dark nights, he became a true wolf boy, as far removed from his previous life as it was possible to be.

Before the crash, the boy had been a brilliant scholar of whom great things were expected. He was already fluent in several European languages and had a passion for history, both ancient and modern. But now, following the head injury that he sustained during the crash, he had no memory of his previous life. Only occasional flashbacks punctuated his feral existence with the wolves and gave him a glimpse of his former life. Although the flashbacks were vivid in their subject matter, the people who featured in them were bereft of distinguishable faces. Otherwise, his mind was intact. He could still remember his languages and his general intelligence was as sharp as a needle.

Then, one morning in March, everything changed. A disgraced Swedish scientist called Nils Ohlson was walking in the forests of Gotland, when he spotted a small pack of wolves. This sighting alone was remarkable, as there were no records of wolves inhabiting the area at this time.

What Nils saw next blew his mind! A teenage boy was running, playing and eating with the wolves – a genuine, twenty-first century wolf boy! At first, Nils could not believe his eyes, but, a quick snapshot with his mobile phone gave him irrefutable proof of the extraordinary find.

'Look at this, Petra!' he exclaimed, bursting into the rented stone tower that now served as their home. 'It could be the answer to all our problems!'

Nils and Petra Ohlson had once lived a comfortable life at Stockholm University where Nils had been a research fellow. Seeing his colleagues gaining promotion around him, but going nowhere himself, he falsified some test results and became a leading light within the scientific community. But, a sharp-eyed Norwegian professor from the neighbouring University of Oslo spotted flaws in his data and published a paper exposing the deceit.

Following an investigation by the university, Nils was duly sacked from his job and forcibly evicted from his luxurious campus house. With his reputation in tatters and with no income, Nils and Petra were forced to take up residence in a draughty stone tower, one of the many set into the medieval walls of Gotland's capital, Visby. It was a terrible comedown and one that Petra never tired of complaining about. Petra was a thin woman with a heart of stone, whose pinched face always looked like she was sucking lemons.

Nils and Petra had a sixteen-year-old son called

Helmar. He was short and stocky with close-cropped hair and, like his mother, had a permanent scowl on his face. Helmar had been badly spoiled in the good times and quickly resorted to violence when he did not get his own way. He cared about no one but himself and was only interested in his powerful, road-racing motorbike.

Desperate to revive the family fortunes, Nils formulated a plan to catch the wolf boy. Armed with a high-voltage stun gun and a box of flares, Nils staked out the area of woodland where he had last seen the feral boy. After several cold days and nights in the driving rain and sleet, Nils found the youth as he feasted on a patch of wild blackberries, while the pack devoured a deer they had killed nearby. Firing the stun gun at point-blank range and then scaring the wolves away with the flares, Nils bundled the shocked boy into his car and drove home, locking him in the empty attic at the top of the tower.

The captured boy's prison was a cold, dirty room

with slit windows that still smelt sickly from the animal skins that had been stored there many years ago. There he was forced to stay, a prisoner against his will.

'I still don't see how we're going to make any money out of this freak,' said Helmar, at breakfast one morning.

'Your father thinks the world will pay a fortune to see the wolf boy of Gotland,' explained Petra.

'I don't just think so, dearest, I know so!' insisted Nils, excitedly pushing back his lank, greasy hair.

'All the other feral children brought up by animals have been youngsters. This one's a teenager, so he must have been with them all his life. That's a first! The newspapers and television stations will be fighting each other for a story like this and will pay a fortune for it. Yes, indeed, Wolfgang is our passport back to fame and fortune!'

'Who?' asked Petra, sharply.

'Wolfgang,' repeated her husband. 'I've decided to call the boy Wolfgang. It means, "there goes the wolf". Clever, don't you think?'

During the long, lonely hours in his draughty stone prison, Wolfgang (as he was now known) tried to come to terms with his current situation and what he could do about it. A repetitive cuckoo calling in the distance provided him with an unlikely source of inspiration. The annoying melody triggered a brief flashback to his former life, giving him an idea. Suddenly, Wolfgang remembered sitting on the sofa late one night, watching an old film on TV. The film was *One Flew Over The Cuckoo's Nest* and the teenager recalled admiring the character of Chief Bromden, an enormous Native American, who pretended to be dumb in order not to give anything away to the authorities. And so, Wolfgang decided to do the same. He did not say a word to his greedy captors, leading them to believe he had not learnt to speak and further confirming their wrong assumption that he had been raised by wolves from birth.

Then, Wolfgang started the howling. For the first

few days, the Ohlsons thought this was just a reaction to captivity and did their best to ignore it. But, as time went on, they began to realise that it was a deliberate ploy to irritate them – and, as far as they were concerned, it proved highly successful.

Wolfgang timed his howls to cause maximum inconvenience and annoyance. He howled at meal times. He howled very early in the morning, waking everyone up. Worst of all, he howled late into the night, making sleep impossible. Nils tried bribes, threats, depriving him of food and all manner of other desperate measures to try and stop the infuriating howling, but their captive took absolutely no notice and carried on regardless.

One rainy night, when Wolfgang had been howling particularly loudly for several hours, Petra finally snapped.

'SHUT UP, SHUT UP, SHUT UP!' she shrieked, holding her head in her hands and rocking violently from side to side. Then, she turned on her husband, grabbing him by the front of his food-stained sweatshirt and shouting hysterically.

'EITHER YOU DO SOMETHING WITH THAT WRETCHED CREATURE, OR I'LL SET HIM FREE!' she snarled.

'Take it easy, my sweet,' replied Nils, freeing himself with an indignant jerk. 'I've just set up a lucrative deal with an American TV company for a two-hour documentary. So, I'll be taking Wolfgang to the States in a few days' time.'

That evening, as a magnificent full moon flooded Wolfgang's prison with celestial light, his former wolf pack made contact with him. Surprisingly, no howling was involved. Instead, Lupe employed an unearthly, animal telepathy to speak directly into Wolfgang's mind. And what the grizzled she-wolf said shocked him to his very core!

'Listen carefully, my son,' she said, speaking slowly and clearly in his native English. 'There is much to tell you and very little time. Everything you're about to hear is true, however far-fetched it may seem. You have been selected for a vital task on which the future of humankind depends … '

'I don't understand,' interrupted Wolfgang, communicating via his thoughts.

'I know you don't,' retorted Lupe with a clear hint of impatience. 'So, please keep listening and I will tell you a true story that could bring about the destruction of the human race …

'About 50,000 years ago, a race of aliens visited Earth with the intention of living here. They travelled in a spaceship powered by the 'Vortex of Light', a triangular prism containing seven objects from different parts of the solar system, each one a different colour of the rainbow. This prism generated enough energy to allow the aliens to travel anywhere in the universe at the speed of light.

'At first, the alien visitors were pleased with where they had landed. Earth was a beautiful, unspoilt place with lots of habitable land, wildlife and plentiful resources. At this time, the only humans were small tribes of hunter-gatherers, who showed great respect for the world in which they lived. Tragically, soon after the aliens' arrival in what is now the Arizona Desert in North America, a natural disaster ruined their plans. A giant meteor struck Earth right beside them and obliterated their spacecraft. In the resulting shockwaves, the precious items from the 'Vortex of Light' were sucked up into the atmosphere and carried around the world, where they eventually fell to Earth and were lost. Those aliens not killed by the strike spent the rest of their lives searching for their missing astral objects and instructing all of the animal species on Earth to look for them too. As the alien survivors died out, their bodies instantly evaporated and left no trace of their existence.

'Now, a new generation of aliens have returned to Earth to reclaim their seven items which, having been left here for so long, have been named the Astral Legacies. On arrival, they were horrified to discover how much the planet had changed in such a comparatively short space of time. Humans had spread around the world and their impact on the

The Astral Legacies
Wolves' Gambit

Written by Gordon Volke

This edition published in Great Britain in 2010 by Quest, an imprint of Top That! Publishing plc,
Marine House, Tide Mill Way, Woodbridge, Suffolk, IP12 1AP, UK
www.quest-books.co.uk
0 2 4 6 8 9 7 5 3 1

Editorial Director – Daniel Graham
Creative Director – Simon Couchman
Art Editor – Matt Denny
Commissioning Editor - Lorna Thomson
Website Design – Paul Strandoo

Written by Gordon Volke

ISBN 978-1-84956-078-8

A catalogue record for this book is available from the British Library
Printed and bound in China

This is a work of fiction. Names, characters, places, incidents and dialogues are products of the author's
imagination or are used fictitiously. Any resemblance to actual people, living or dead, events or locales is
entirely coincidental.

The Astral Legacies
Wolves' Gambit

Written by Gordon Volke

For Karen

Published by Quest.
Quest is an imprint of Top That! Publishing plc,
Tide Mill Way, Woodbridge, Suffolk, IP12 1AP, UK
www.quest-books.co.uk
Copyright © 2010 Top That! Publishing plc.

How the book works ...

Join Wolfgang in his quest to find the third Astral Legacy by searching for the hidden locations online. At key points in the book, the wolves provide Wolfgang with precise information relating to the destinations that he must visit in order to complete his quest. Each GPS (Global Positioning System) coordinate that is transmitted by the wolves represents a precise location in Europe.

By entering the GPS coordinates into the GeoLocator function on **www.astrallegacies.com**, you will be able to travel with Wolfgang on his quest. Click the wolf icon on the revolving carousel, then select the 'GeoLocator' link to begin. For example, try these coordinates – they will take you to the Parthenon in Athens, Greece:

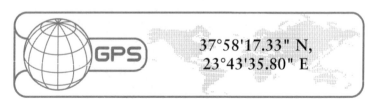

GPS

37°58'17.33" N,
23°43'35.80" E

When you 'arrive' at each new destination online, you will discover the famous landmark that Wolfgang is seeking.

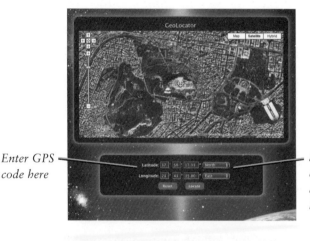

Enter GPS code here

Select compass direction here

Use this slider to zoom in and see the location in more detail

Explore the area in more detail by clicking here

Click on the red arrow to reveal the location

As the adventure unfolds, keep a note of the locations that you find. When you have identified all ten key locations that Wolfgang visits on his quest, enter the words that make up each location into the 'crossword' grid at the back of this book. If you have inserted the correct answers, the location of the third Astral Legacy will be revealed, highlighted in grey.

Log-on to **www.astrallegacies.com** to report the location of the third Astral Legacy. If you successfully enter this final landmark, the quest is complete and you will be able to read the thrilling climax to *Wolves' Gambit.*

Once you have completed the crossword, the letters highlighted in grey, spell out the location of the third Astral Legacy.

Important Hints & Tips

• Enter the GPS coordinates accurately, including the compass direction.

• Use the 'Notes' section at the back of this book to record the locations that you identify as you progress through the quest. You will then have everything at hand to complete the 'crossword' puzzle at the end of the book and finish the quest with Wolfgang.

• The wolves have provided additional clues to help you fill in the crossword correctly at the back of this book.

Chapter 1

Howling at the Moon

'Mayday! Mayday!' shouted the panicked pilot of Flight 107 as it plummeted towards the Baltic Sea. 'Bird-strike in both engines. We've lost all power ...'

The message ended abruptly as the aircraft struck the inky black water, breaking in half on impact.

*   *   *   *   *   *   *   *   *   *   *

Tragically, after a lengthy search-and-rescue operation, the authorities concluded that there were no survivors from the plane crash and that many of the bodies would never be recovered. But, they were wrong! A fifteen-year-old English boy had been thrown clear of the wreckage and, banging his head on the edge of the wing, somersaulted into the turbulent sea. The life-jacket he had been made to put on minutes before the crash kept him afloat and environment was disastrous – habitats destroyed, animals extinct, widespread pollution and ever-increasing global warming. Having heard stories from their ancestors about how idyllic Earth was before, the aliens wanted to reverse this trend by exterminating the entire human race. Fortunately, the wiser heads among them pointed out that such a punishment would be grossly unfair. Only the older generation of human beings were responsible for these terrible crimes – the young are innocent. So, a compromise was agreed.

'The aliens promised to leave Earth alone, provided that their seven Astral Legacies are returned. Seven young people, chosen at random, would be given the task of finding the objects within a single calendar year. Two chosen children have already succeeded in their quests. A North American boy and an Indian girl have located and returned the missing astral objects from their respective continents. You have been chosen to find the third one in Europe ...'

At that point, Helmar and Petra barged in with Wolfgang's supper, interrupting the message.

'Not howling tonight, Wolf Boy?' scoffed Helmar.

'Be quiet, you idiot,' snapped his mother, cuffing her son round the back of his head. 'We don't want to tempt fate!'

When his captors had gone, Wolfgang was eager to resume communication with the wolves, but there was total silence. After an agonising wait, Lupe got in touch with him again just before dawn the following morning.

'I've given you time to digest what I told you last night,' she said, in a brisk, business-like fashion. 'We, your wolf-brethren, are the chosen animal guardians of the third Astral Legacy and we will help you to escape from your prison. When you are free, we will provide you with the global positioning coordinates of ten places within the continent of Europe. You must visit each one in turn, noting down the names of the chosen sites. When you have collected all ten names, we will instruct you on how to combine them, in order to reveal the secret location of the third Astral Legacy.'

'Why can't I ...?' began Wolfgang, but the she-wolf anticipated what he was going to say.

'You can't just go straight to the final location because this is a test that you have to pass. The aliens want to be sure that the people of Earth are worth saving and, to illustrate that, your courage and resourcefulness must be stretched to the very limit. During your time with my pack you have already proven that you are worthy of the responsibility that has been forced upon you.'

'What else do I need to know?' asked Wolfgang, suddenly eager to get started.

'You must keep your quest an absolute secret,' advised Lupe. 'Tell no one, however lonely you may feel or however tempted you are to share your burden. Above all, remember this is not a game and failure is not an option. Your quest is a matter of life and death, not just for you, but for everyone on this planet. If you, or any of the other chosen children, do not find the Astral Legacies within the allotted time, the human race will be wiped out at a stroke!'

Wolfgang was still reeling at the terrifying responsibility being placed on his young shoulders when Lupe's telepathic briefing abruptly ended. The sudden silence left him feeling empty and confused. He longed to know how he was going to escape, but he trusted his wolf family and knew that they would free him when the time was right.

Once the shock had subsided, the thought of being free changed his mood and sent his spirits soaring. As dawn broke, Wolfgang woke the whole household with a chorus of howling that was not his usual melancholy wail. This time, his howl was full of undisguised joy and excitement.

Chapter 2

Red in Tooth and Claw

Nils Ohlson's pride and joy was his car, a glossy black convertible bought just a few days before he was ousted from the university. Petra and Helmar were always nagging him to sell it, but he refused. Nils loved to polish it on a Sunday morning and then drive it around the narrow streets of Visby, giving the impression that he was still a rich and important person. He also loved playing with the gadgets, especially the state-of-the-art satellite navigation system. It was detachable to prevent theft and, if it was stolen, it had an inbuilt tracking device that sent out a signal, allowing its location to be traced.

Wolfgang was sitting in the back of this car, on the first leg of his journey to America, when he saw the first wolf running along the hilltop above. As the journey progressed, he witnessed several other ghost-like shadows out of the corner of his eye. His wolf pack were stalking the car. Excitement rippled through Wolfgang's body like electricity. He sat bolt upright, eager to witness what events would unfold.

It seemed an eternity before the pack made their next move, and the manner of it shocked and saddened Wolfgang. An elderly wolf, that he knew was sick, ran out in front of the car as it turned a narrow corner on the hilly road. WHUMP! Wolfgang closed his eyes to avoid seeing the impact. Observing the lifeless body of his wolf brother at the side of the road, Wolfgang knew that it was time to act. As Nils got out to inspect the dead wolf, swearing furiously at the damage to his car, Wolfgang wiped tears from his eyes and made his escape.

His breakout was spotted a split-second later, but it was already too late. The wolves, led by Lupe, appeared from out of the trees on either side of the road, snarling and growling menacingly. They surrounded Nils and kept him prisoner as Wolfgang opened the boot of the car to collect what he needed for his journey. From the suitcase, reluctantly packed for him by Petra, he took his toothbrush, a change of clothes and a puzzle book and pen. Then, he rifled through the pockets of Nils's jacket, taking his passport, driving licence and wallet containing some cash and an array of credit cards. Finally, he detached the satnav system so he could use it to find the locations given to him by the wolves. Unbeknown to Wolfgang, the unit immediately commenced sending out a silent tracking pulse that would make his quest more perilous than he could ever have imagined.

With the items collected, and neatly stowed in a small rucksack, Wolfgang felt a tide of panic sweeping through his body. What was he supposed to do now? Run down the road on foot? Hitch a lift from the next passer-by? Steal a bicycle?

Fortunately, at that moment, a strong smell of petrol wafted from the dented bonnet of Nils's car, triggering a vivid flashback in his mind.

Suddenly, the crash scene vanished and Wolfgang could see himself back on his grandfather's farm. He was driving an old van round and round a rutted private road, waving to onlookers and laughing with glee. That was it! He knew how to drive! He could take the car!

The look on Nils's face as Wolfgang jumped into the driver's seat of his beloved car was priceless. It felt even better when Wolfgang looked in his rear-view mirror and saw his captor being chased into the forest by the wolves. With adrenaline coursing through his veins, Wolfgang started the engine. The open road lay ahead of him and his quest had begun!

* * * * * * * * * * *

Standing on the deck of the ferry as it crossed from Gotland to the Swedish mainland, Wolfgang decided to get rid of the convertible. There was still a lot of blood on the front bumper and, every time he looked at it, he felt an overwhelming sense of sadness at the sacrifice made by his wolf brother. So, once on the mainland, he drove straight to a second-hand car dealership where he swapped the conspicuous convertible for an anonymous-looking hatchback and a small amount of cash.

Wolfgang's next stop was a photobooth at Stockholm railway station, where he took a strip of pictures of himself. Then, he carefully substituted them in place of Nils's photographs in the stolen passport and driving licence. Wolfgang had no recollection of travelling abroad, and yet he knew that these important documents would be required in order to travel and withdraw money from Nils's bank accounts. Indeed, with each passing day, Wolfgang found that many other useful skills and memories from his old life came flooding back to him.

The forgery was something of a gamble, due to the massive age difference between himself and the account owner. Wolfgang was concerned that an official would spot the discrepancy between the date of birth and the photo. But, it was a risk he needed to take if he was to complete the vital quest.

Walking along the riverbank to the city centre, Wolfgang could feel the perspiration gathering on his brow and in the small of his back. As he stepped into the first bank he was convinced that he would be found out and turned over to the police. Wolfgang was astonished when the cashiers raised no objections, other than requesting a routine look at his documents, before giving him Nils's money. By visiting all of the branches, one by one, and only taking out a small sum of money each time, he had enough cash to travel right around Europe in the coming weeks.

As Wolfgang hurried back to his car, he felt a tingling sensation in his hand and the wolves provided him with the coordinates of his first destination:

GPS 1   55°41'34.20" N,
         12°35'57.50" E

Not trusting himself to remember these vital letters and numbers, he took the puzzle book and pen out of his rucksack and scribbled them down on the blank inside back cover. Then, quickly typing the numbers and letters into the satnav system, he found out where he needed to go.

The journey south from Sweden to Denmark was uneventful. Being an inexperienced driver, Wolfgang drove slowly and carefully, mindful that the success of his quest and the safety of others depended on him not having an accident. However, he soon got the feel of the road and, as the Friday night traffic slowly petered out, he took to the motorway and drove through the night while it was quiet.

Tired and stiff and more than a little hungry, Wolfgang rolled through the outskirts of Copenhagen early the following morning. Following the signs, he made his way towards the harbour and parked his car near a café in the beautiful Langelinie Park that bordered the sea. The tantalising smell of fresh coffee wafted out to him from a nearby café, making him long for breakfast, but he ignored the pangs in his stomach and hurried on to complete the first leg of his quest.

The well signposted path to Copenhagen's most famous tourist attraction took him along the water's edge to a rounded rock jutting out into the sea. Like thousands of other visitors before him, the size of the bronze statue took him by surprise. It was only just over a metre tall, small for a figure that was an iconic image of the Danish capital and known all around the world. The statue was very beautiful and Wolfgang was gazing admiringly at its form when the wolves contacted him with a second set of coordinates:

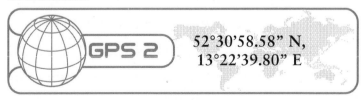

GPS 2

52°30'58.58" N,
13°22'39.80" E

Wolfgang was startled at the immediacy of their communication. But, despite this swift prompting, he knew it would be dangerous to continue his quest straight away. He desperately needed some food and some sleep. So, he hurried back to the café and ordered croissant rolls with jam and coffee.

Afterwards, Wolfgang felt much better and headed back to his car with a view to enjoying a rest on the back seat before moving on to his next destination.

His eyes were already growing heavy as he reached the car park, but they jerked wide open when he saw whose motorbike was parked right next to his car. It was Helmar's! Wolfgang had often looked down through the narrow windows of his attic prison and watched enviously as the thug raced around on it. Clearly, the Ohlsons' son had followed him with a view to getting him back, but how did he know where to find him? It was a baffling mystery that Wolfgang was still trying to fathom out when he felt a big hand clamp down painfully on his shoulder.

'Hello, Wolfie!' chortled Helmar. 'You're coming with me!' Wolfgang said nothing in reply, but instinctively stamped hard on Helmar's foot, feeling the heel of his new shoes crushing his tormentor's toes. Helmar bellowed in pain and immediately released his grip on Wolfgang, who was forced to flee from the car park with the irate figure of Helmar hobbling painfully after him.

Once outside the park, the cityscape became much more like a dockland with wharves and storage warehouses filling the narrow streets and alleyways, many of them cul-de-sacs. Wolfgang took full advantage of his ability to run faster than his adversary and soon lost Helmar among the maze of tall buildings. Feeling elated, Wolfgang headed back to his car, but, in a careless moment he took a wrong turning and followed the road to a dead end. As he turned to retrace his steps, he saw the menacing figure of Helmar blocking the exit and limping menacingly towards him. There was no escape! Wolfgang would have to fight his way out of the alley and Helmar had no intention of making it a fair contest. As the stocky Swedish bully approached, he picked up an iron bar from a rubbish skip and dragged it malevolently across the wall as he approached.

Just as sights and smells had triggered flashbacks to his former life, the fact of being backed into a corner caused Wolfgang to instinctively revert to wolf-like behaviour. The transformation was terrifying as Wolfgang began snarling and showing his teeth, causing Helmar to hesitate at first. But, it was not enough to deter him. The bully knew that he would be in for a share of the profits if he managed to recapture the family's ticket to fame and fortune, so he marched forwards and whacked Wolfgang across the shoulder with the iron bar.

'And there's plenty more where that came from, Wolf Boy!' he shouted. 'So, you'd better come quietly.'

Submission was not an option, so Wolfgang

launched himself at Helmar in a furious, snarling, counter-attack.

The famous Victorian poet, Alfred Lord Tennyson, once described nature as being 'red in tooth and claw'. This would also make a very apt description of the violent fight that ensued between Wolfgang and Helmar. Wrenching the iron bar out of his rival's grip, Wolfgang threw it aside, where it landed on the pavement with a deafening clang. Then, he dodged around to the other side of his opponent, boxing him into the corner.

Outmanoeuvred and overwhelmed by the speed of Wolfgang's attack, the Swede found himself repeatedly bitten and scratched by his former captive. Before long, Helmar was defeated and, unable to take any more, he pushed Wolfgang aside and fled. Dropping to all fours and loping back along the grubby pavement of the cul-de-sac, Wolfgang pursued his assailant to ensure victory. Anyone watching the fight would have thought that a real wolf was prowling the streets of Copenhagen.

Then, it was over. Shaking his head, as if coming out of a trance, Wolfgang heard the roar of Helmar's motorbike and saw him speeding down the road, no doubt heading for a hospital – his wounds would need stitching and disinfecting. Not that this bothered Wolfgang in the slightest. Having licked his own cuts and bruises clean in true wolf-fashion, he jumped into his car and drove out of Copenhagen.

Once on the motorway, he pulled into the nearest service station, where he parked up and slept until lunchtime, completely oblivious to all of the cars and heavy lorries thundering past him.

Chapter 3

Run, Rabbit, Run

As he approached Berlin early on Sunday morning, Wolfgang felt good. The sun was shining, the autobahn was quiet and he'd just had a magnificent breakfast at a spotlessly clean motorway service station. Best of all, he had seen off Helmar and could continue on his quest without the spectre of the Swedish bully snapping at his heels.

The outskirts of the German capital were surprisingly pleasant. Wolfgang had expected a long, urban sprawl of streets and houses like those around London, but he found himself driving through a mixture of woodland and lakes that looked as picturesque as anything in a travel brochure. The River Spree, on which the German capital is situated, flashed invitingly in the distance as the bright, early morning sunshine reflected from its silvery waters.

'This is the life!' chuckled Wolfgang to himself,

comparing the surrounding beauty with his days cooped up in the revolting stone attic.

However, Wolfgang's merriment was short-lived, as the unmistakable visage of Helmar appeared in his rear-view mirror, looking like an overweight Power Ranger in his all-in-one leather bodysuit, gauntlets and gaudily-painted helmet. Helmar's body language made his intentions quite clear. He sat stiffly on his motorbike, shoulders hunched, aggression and determination radiating from every muscle.

'How the hell did he know where to find me?' exclaimed Wolfgang, not realising that his pursuer was picking up the stolen satnav signal on his iPhone and instantly locating its whereabouts to within a couple of metres. But, there was no time to ponder on this any further. Helmar overtook Wolfgang with a roar of acceleration and cut in front of him, pointing urgently at the hard shoulder like a policeman pulling in a suspect.

'You'll be lucky,' cried Wolfgang, putting his foot

down on the accelerator and almost knocking his enemy off the road.

Weaving in and out of the traffic, a high speed chase began, in which Wolfgang tried unsuccessfully to outrun his rival. His car was not built for speed, whereas Helmar was riding a high-powered motorbike that would be quite at home in a Grand Prix race. Wolfgang soon realised he could not win a straightforward race, so he would have to resort to wolf-like cunning instead.

As they entered the city, stopping and starting at numerous traffic lights, Wolfgang timed it so that he crossed the lights just as they changed to red, causing Helmar to make several screeching emergency stops. On the first occasion, the desperate Swede jumped the lights and nearly collided with a bus coming from the right. Next time, he was forced to skid to a halt to avoid going right underneath a huge delivery truck.

So, Wolfgang got away for a few precious seconds and, in that time, managed to duck down a side road and out of sight. After waiting ages for the coast to clear, Wolfgang drove into the city centre, and left his car in a multi-storey car park, before making his way to his second destination on foot.

Whereas the statue in Copenhagen harbour had been surprisingly small, this monument in the west of Berlin was breathtakingly huge. Its twelve massive columns towered above Wolfgang's head, making him feel very insignificant. At the same time, he felt excited at the thought that he was standing on the very spot crossed by Napoleon, as he entered and left the city. No wonder this magnificent monument was a national symbol that appeared on one of the German banknotes.

A few moments after his first sighting of the landmark, the wolves contacted him with his next set of coordinates:

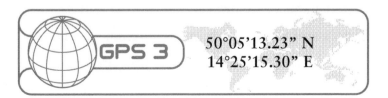

GPS 3

50°05'13.23" N
14°25'15.30" E

After jotting down the numbers and letters, Wolfgang was now faced with a dilemma. Should he carry straight on with his quest and risk being caught up in the busy daytime traffic? Or, should he wait until nightfall when it would be less congested and easier to sneak away? He decided on the latter option, which meant he could spend the rest of the day in Berlin.

Fortunately, the cobblestone pedestrian zone around the monument was rapidly filling up with officials and competitors preparing for a charity fun run that afternoon. It looked like a really big event, so Wolfgang decided to stick with the crowds in the hope that he would not be spotted by his persistent assailant. In the meantime, he decided to seek out a mid-morning treat of coffee and cake.

There were plenty of places where he could find such delights. The famous avenue of lime trees, Unter den Linden, began at the monument and boasted many fine cafés. So did the Tiergarten, an enormous tree-lined park that stretched away as far as the eye could see in the opposite direction. Wolfgang chose the park and wandered into an immaculately clean, self-service restaurant. Feeling ravenously hungry, he bought a coffee and two enormous cakes – a long eclair with thick chocolate on the top and a round meringue; its crispy white sides were glued together with lots of double cream.

The café was next to a wide avenue, down which runners in fancy dress and spectators poured in ever-increasing numbers. Wolfgang thought he'd sit outside to watch this colourful procession while he enjoyed his food. There was a space at a corner table whose only other occupant was a man reading a newspaper, which he held up in front of his face.

'Is that for me?' asked the man in Swedish.

'I beg your pardon?' exclaimed Wolfgang, startled by such rudeness.

'You've bought two cakes,' continued the voice from behind the newspaper. 'I wondered if one of them was for me?'

'No, of course not … ' began Wolfgang,

indignantly.

Then, his jaw dropped open in disbelief as the man slowly lowered the newspaper. Helmar was sitting right opposite him, grinning like one of the gargoyles that guarded many of the gothic buildings in the surrounding area.

Wolfgang shot away from the café like a sprinter at the start of an Olympic final. Helmar tore after him, determined not to let his quarry escape this time. Both of them ignored the angry shouts from people who were nearly knocked over or forced to leap aside by the frantic pursuit. Down one crowded tree-arched path and along another they charged; Wolfgang just managing to keep far enough ahead to avoid being grabbed.

Then, Helmar played his trump card. He was a keen rugby player (often cited for violent conduct) and was an expert at the flying rugby tackle. So, just as Wolfgang was starting to slip out of reach, Helmar launched himself forwards in a spectacular dive and locked his arms around the English boy's legs. Wolfgang crashed to the ground with a cry of surprise and pain and, seconds later, Helmar was standing over him with a demonic grin of triumph etched on his face.

'Get up, Wolf Boy!' he snarled.

Pretending to be more badly hurt than he was, Wolfgang groaned as he rolled over onto his back. Then, like a martial arts expert, he shot out his right foot and caught Helmar in the chest, sending him flying backwards, with his arms flailing around on either side. By the time the Swede had scrambled to his feet, Wolfgang had disappeared into the dense crowd now thronging the pedestrian plaza for the start of the race. Still winded, Helmar was unable to catch up with Wolfgang, and watched as his elusive catch headed in the direction of the race hire fancy dress kiosk, before being swallowed up by the crowd.

*   *   *   *   *   *   *   *   *   *   *

At one o'clock sharp, the BANG of the starting pistol signalled the beginning of the event. By now, hundreds of runners and thousands of spectators were thronging the route, shouting and cheering as they enjoyed the sunshine and the lively carnival atmosphere. Many of the runners were already regretting their choice of costume, sweltering inside their clown suits or furry animal costumes.

Helmar stood some way down the line, scanning the passing runners for Wolfgang. Then, to his delight, a runner in a wolf costume appeared near the end of the line, as would befit a sudden last-minute entry. When the furry grey figure drew level, Helmar launched himself from the crowd with a banshee-like yell and knocked the runner to the ground.

Roughly yanking off the wolf mask, Helmar expected to see Wolfgang staring up at him, his face ashen with fear. Instead, he saw a red-faced German woman glaring up at him with a face like thunder. Helmar began to stammer a few apologies, but the burly female runner took no notice and leapt to her feet, seething with rage. Without saying a word, she grabbed hold of Helmar's shirt, lifted him right off the ground and carried him, arms and legs flailing, to a nearby fountain. Then, she dropped him into the water, like someone depositing a piece of unpleasant rubbish into a dustbin.

A few moments later, as the dripping thug struggled out of the fountain, much to the amusement of the spectators, a brown rabbit with a fluffy white tail and one bent-over ear came jogging past, giving an enthusiastic thumbs-up sign of approval.

Chapter 4

My Kingdom for a Horse

Helmar didn't follow Wolfgang as he made his way down through southern Germany into the Czech Republic. Instead, he overtook him on the autobahn, roaring past like a two-wheeled Teutonic Knight, slowing momentarily to pull a bare-bottomed moon.

'He's so confident!' sighed Wolfgang, who was beginning to think that his rival must have some kind of amazing psychic ability. Whatever method Helmar was using to track him, there was nothing he could do about it, other than to continue with the quest. Part of him hoped that the wolves might intervene and tell him Helmar's secret, but, of course, there was no contact.

'Okay, guys,' murmured Wolfgang. 'I know the rules.'

The reason Helmar had sped on ahead was to

catch up with two friends living in Prague, whose help he wanted to enlist in catching Wolfgang. They were a pair of violent thugs whom Helmar had hung out with at school before they were expelled.

Their names were Hans and Lars Gustavson and they were identical twins. Their blank, shark-like eyes and sharp facial features were strikingly similar, however, Hans was clean cut with long, wavy hair and a smart line of suits, and Lars had a shaven head, a nose-ring, and tattoos snaking up his arms. Both were dangerous, but in different ways. Hans, who was the brains of the outfit, was cool and calculating and relished being cruel. His twin, Lars, on the other hand, liked to use his fists, before putting what little brain he had into gear. Together they were a destructive force to be reckoned with!

The brothers lived in a disgusting squat in the back streets of the Czechoslovakian capital. The wallpaper was peeling off the walls, the carpets were a grimy shade of black and the toilet only flushed when the chain was yanked suddenly, taking it by surprise.

'Nice place you've got here,' said Helmar, sarcastically.

'Yeah, cool, innit?' agreed Lars, perfectly seriously.

The twins both wanted to know all about Wolfgang, and grew visibly excited at the prospect of getting their hands on him and having some fun.

'I gotta take him back in one piece, guys,' stressed Helmar, suddenly anxious that his friends might overdo the heavy stuff.

'Don't worry, buddy-boy, our handiwork won't show,' chuckled Hans, slapping Helmar hard on the shoulder. 'So, where do we find your hairy, little pal?'

'He should be arriving in the centre of town round about now,' replied Helmar, looking at his wristwatch.

'How on earth do you know that?' asked Lars.

'I have my methods,' chuckled their visitor, arrogantly tapping the side of his nose with one finger.

In fact, had Helmar made another tracking check on his iPhone, he would have discovered that Wolfgang was still some distance from his destination, the Old Town Square. He was stuck in traffic that had gridlocked the centre of Prague. It was the beginning of the Easter holidays and many tourists were flocking to the 'City of a Hundred Spires' on day trips and package holidays. In the end, a frustrated Wolfgang had turned out of the queues and followed signs to a back-street car park, where he was lucky enough to find a space straight away. Carefully noting the name and location of the car park, Wolfgang hurried through the maze of ancient, narrow streets until he reached the spot he needed to find; the southern wall of the Old Town Hall in the Square.

Wolfgang had enjoyed visiting his first two locations and he liked this one even more. It was an amazing feat of medieval engineering that appealed to his great love of history. He gazed at the huge dials and watched, fascinated, as the big clockwork figures appeared and disappeared with the passage of time. It came as something of an irritation when he felt the now-familiar sensation in his hand as the wolves contacted him once more, but he carefully noted down the coordinates of his fourth destination, knowing perfectly well that he was not on holiday:

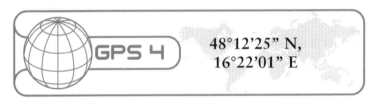

GPS 4

48°12'25" N,
16°22'01" E

Wolfgang spotted Helmar and his two accomplices as he turned to leave the square. They stood together on a street corner, surveying the area like giant meerkats. Wolfgang felt cold beads of sweat breaking out on his forehead as they spotted him and started to head menacingly towards him.

Wolfgang took off like a lone, marauding wolf being chased by Akbash, the huge, determined guard dogs bred by Turkish farmers to protect their flocks of sheep. His only hope was to use the ever-increasing crowds of tourists as cover. But, wherever he chose to go, one of the trio would always turn up a few moments later and threaten to catch him.

He tried milling with the shoppers browsing the colourful souvenir stalls on Charles Bridge, the ancient and picturesque crossing-point of the River Vltava. But, Lars blocked his path and would have caught Wolfgang had he not barged into an off-duty fire officer who pushed him back like a puppet, sending him sprawling into a display of leather handbags.

Gratefully making his escape, Wolfgang ducked back into Prague Castle, one of the largest stone castles in the world, where he took refuge in the toy museum. Unfortunately, it was only a matter of time before Hans came snooping around, fixing Wolfgang with a cold, calculating stare through one of the glass exhibit cabinets. Quickly slipping out of an open side door, the now-tiring Wolfgang hurried to Wenceslas Square, in the heart of the city, where he hoped that the crowds would conceal him. He stood, breathless and sweating, under the statue of an ancient saint, the Duke of Bohemia (907–935), whose name is known worldwide, thanks to the Christmas carol, 'Good King Wenceslas'.

Suddenly, despite all of the danger, Wolfgang experienced another flashback. He remembered Christmas at home with his family, and how he had substituted the lame jokes in their lunchtime crackers with some clever ones of his own. Although he could not recall their faces, a smile broke out on his face as he reminisced on how much everyone had laughed at his favourite festive joke:

'Good King Wenceslas walked into his local pizza shop. "My usual, please," he said. "Deep pan, crisp and even."'

The smile soon faded from Wolfgang's face as he saw Helmar, barging roughly through the crowds like someone wading through water. It would only be a matter of seconds before he was spotted, and what would he do then? Exhausted following the long chase, he turned over all sorts of crazy possibilities in his mind: alert the police by causing a disturbance; pretend to collapse and get taken to hospital; change his appearance by stealing clothes from a shop; but, a far simpler solution arrived right under his nose in the form of a taxi that stopped directly in front of him. The roof-light was shining to show that the cab was free, so Wolfgang simply tapped on the window and then jumped into the back seat, asking to be taken to the car park where he had left his car.

The dour taxi-driver was none too pleased at making such a short journey, so Wolfgang offered to pay him double in order to make a quick escape. Five minutes later, the weary fugitive climbed into his car and headed out of Prague, leaving his three pursuers getting increasingly frustrated and quarrelsome as they searched the busy streets in vain.

Whilst travelling the short distance from Prague to Austria, Wolfgang started to feel the strain of his quest for the first time. The novelty of being free and driving the car had long since worn off. He was tired of sleeping on the cramped back seat and eating at irregular times, often having to bolt his food or leave it unfinished because he had to hurry away. However, the most stressful part of his quest was that Helmar was always there, right behind him, no matter where he went or what he did. Wolfgang longed for the peace and quiet that he enjoyed with his adoptive wolf family back in Gotland.

'Maybe I'll find some time to relax in Vienna,' he mused.

* * * * * * * * * * *

The latest set of coordinates took Wolfgang right into the heart of Vienna, to the magnificent Hofburg Imperial Palace. There were many different parts to the enormous building, but Wolfgang headed straight for a large, white hall with tall windows. The hall exterior was covered with posters boasting that the most prestigious equestrian centre in the world lay within. Frustratingly, there was no response from the wolves as Wolfgang stood outside, so he paid for a ticket and went in.

Once inside, Wolfgang was marshalled to a seated gallery, where members of the public could watch the horses being trained. They were special Lipizzan horses who, through years of careful schooling, had learnt to make graceful movements in perfect time to music. Wolfgang had always disliked this type of formal dressage, thinking it utterly pointless and something of an insult to the horses' intelligence. Then, he learnt from a guidebook that all of the moves were originally devised to strengthen the horses' bodies and train their minds to make them supreme in battle. Suddenly, the well-rehearsed drills made sense, and he began to admire the tireless effort and amazing skill that went into such perfectly controlled movements.

Wolfgang was so lost in watching the performance of a ballerina-esque grey mare that he nearly missed the next communication from the wolves. Grabbing the puzzle book and pen from his rucksack, he jotted the numbers and letters down:

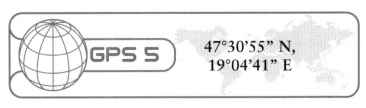

GPS 5

47°30'55" N,
19°04'41" E

'What are you doing?' asked a gentle voice beside him. Wolfgang looked round and found that he was sitting next to a German girl about his own age. She had long, fair hair tied back in a ponytail and a rounded, friendly-looking face. Her outfit consisted of a checked shirt, tight jeans and black knee-length leather boots with a brow top, making it clear that she was keen on riding.

'Just taking a few notes,' he replied casually,

switching effortlessly into her language.

There was a long, awkward pause. Then, Wolfgang blurted out, 'Do you come here often?' It was such a corny line, that they both burst out laughing and the ice was broken.

Wolfgang wanted to know more about his cheerful new companion, but she only told him that her name was Lotte, and then seemed quite happy just to sit beside him. The comfortable silence suited Wolfgang. So, the pair sat watching the horses perform, occasionally glancing across at each other and smiling. As the day wore on, a friendship was kindled with barely a word being spoken.

When the horses had finished performing, the new friends went to get a drink. However, their peace and quiet was soon shattered when a scruffy-looking Helmar stormed in through the front entrance, sporting a black eye and a badly swollen lip. He had parted company on bad terms with his unsavoury buddies, who had not taken kindly to spending a long, hot day on a wild goose chase around the streets of Prague. Wolfgang also noticed the murderous expression on Helmar's face and, acting purely on instinct, hurried away, leaving Lotte on her own.

'Hey! Where are you going?' cried Lotte, in a surprised voice. This attracted Helmar's attention and he charged over, knocking her aside and racing off in hot pursuit of Wolfgang. Amidst shouts of anger from the equestrian officials and other visitors, Wolfgang and Helmar charged around the lobby and out through the front entrance.

Refreshed after his brief period of relaxation, Wolfgang just managed to dodge around the left-hand side of the building before his enemy emerged and thundered off in search of him to the right.

The lull gave Lotte time to find her strange new friend. She hurried up to him as he stood leaning forwards, hands on knees.

'Are you okay? Did he hurt you?' Wolfgang asked, gasping for breath.

'I'm fine,' she replied, brushing off Wolfgang's

concern. 'You're in trouble, aren't you?' she
continued. 'How can I help?'

At first, Wolfgang was inclined to dismiss her
kind offer, but then a wild idea came into his head.

'Can you drive?' he asked.

'Yes, I passed my test two months ago,' she
proudly replied.

'And you really want to help me, even though
it might be dangerous?' he queried, needing to
make sure.

'Of course!' she answered, the earnest look in
her eyes making it quite clear that she meant what
she said.

'Right then, put this on,' said Wolfgang, taking
off his battered jacket and handing it to her along
with his car keys.

'I want you to pretend to be me. Please, take my
car – it's a yellow hatchback with a Swedish
number plate – and drive it out of the city. That
thug will follow you on his motorbike. If he catches
up with you, stay inside the car because he'll go into

meltdown when he finds out that he's been tricked. If the plan works, it'll give me enough time to get to the station and escape on the train.'

'So, I won't see you again?' she whispered, tears welling up in her eyes.

'Of course you will!' exclaimed Wolfgang, taking hold of both of her hands. 'I'll meet you back here at exactly the same time next year ... if we're saved.'

'What do you mean, "if we're saved"?' she queried.

'I'll explain everything to you then,' he called, kissing her briefly on the forehead and hurrying away.

Full of emotion and keen to make his escape, Wolfgang clumsily ran straight into a team of security guards, who were furious that the peace and quiet of their hallowed institution had been so rudely shattered. Two of the guards were already holding Helmar, with his arms pinned behind his back. Two more yelled at Wolfgang and, when he refused to stop, raced after him. Fortunately, the guards, who rarely had anything to do, were not very fit and the teenager soon lost them in the maze of buildings surrounding the area. Dodging round a corner, Wolfgang found himself in a courtyard of an extensive stable block.

In Shakepeare's play, *Richard III*, the king is desperate to escape from his defeat at the Battle of Bosworth and shouts, 'A horse! A horse! My kingdom for a horse!'

Wolfgang found himself in much the same position, only he had a whole line of horses facing him, gazing peacefully out of their half-doors. Another daring plan flashed into Wolfgang's mind. He would make his getaway by borrowing a horse!

Putting on a riding jacket and a hard hat taken from a peg inside one of the doors, Wolfgang led out a delicate chestnut filly who looked about the right size for him. The creak of the leather saddle and the jingle of her bridle triggered another vivid flashback to his former life. Wolfgang recalled being on his grandad's farm, hacking around a small sandy ring on a sturdy pony called Toots. The memory caused a surge of energy to flood through his anxious body. He could do this! He knew how to ride!

Wolfgang skilfully pulled himself up onto the horse's back, just as the two security guards skidded around the corner of the stable block and headed towards him. Digging his heels into the animal's flanks, he shot forward like a racehorse coming out of the starting stalls. In a few short strides, he built up enough speed to leap right over the heads of the security guards, knocking one onto a pile of manure and another into a water trough. Then, he was away, cantering through the car park and jumping the fence into the extensive grounds of the palace. Exhilarated, Wolfgang galloped across the well-kept lawns, relishing the speed and power of the animal beneath him, and headed for a small gate that led to the street beyond. Dismounting, he gave his mount a grateful pat on the neck and set her to graze, before hurrying out of the gate and heading for

Vienna Central Station.

Wolfgang had not gone far when he saw his
small, yellow car speeding away from the equestrian
centre with his disguised friend crouching behind
the wheel. Moments later, Helmar came thundering
along on his motorbike in dogged pursuit. Wolfgang
felt a stab of wild excitement as he witnessed his
plan in action. Having escaped from the security
guards by brute force, Helmar was almost blind
with rage at the sight of his nemesis escaping once
again. Frantically, Helmar swerved in and out of the
fast-moving traffic in an attempt to catch up with
Wolfgang's car.

Wolfgang heard the CRASH as he started on his
journey to the station. Horrified at the thought
that Lotte might be hurt, he hurried to the scene,
but instead saw his deadly rival pinned underneath
his heavy machine, with one leg sticking out at an
unnatural angle. It was obviously broken and
Wolfgang felt a brief moment of pity for his
defeated enemy. These emotions quickly gave way

to an overwhelming sense of elation when he realised that the chase was finally over and he could get on with the remainder of his quest in peace.

Chapter 5

A Lesson in Chess

Before leaving Vienna, Wolfgang went to buy
himself some new clothes. He chose a white tee shirt
and a blue denim jacket that he hoped would make
him look ordinary. He also bought himself a pair of
trainers to replace the uncomfortable black shoes he
had been made to wear by the Ohlsons. The shop
assistant served Wolfgang with a clear element of
distaste, often turning his head away and tutting.
Wolfgang put this down to snobbery, as he had
chosen an upmarket sports shop on the concourse
of Vienna station.

Sitting on the comfortable, modern train as it
headed south on its scenic journey to Budapest in
Hungary, Wolfgang felt relaxed for the first time in
ages. He bought himself some tasty food from the
buffet car and sat eating it, gazing out of the
window at the green fields, shimmering lakes and

distant mountains that went flashing by in rapid succession. The fact that Helmar was no longer pursuing him felt like a great weight had been lifted from his shoulders.

'There must have been an anti-theft tracking device in that car I bought,' he thought to himself. 'Maybe that's how he kept on my tail. Well, that's gone now, so I'm safe!'

Tired after his many high-octane encounters with Helmar, Wolfgang closed his eyes and quickly dozed off to sleep. The train began to get busier as it neared Budapest and as Wolfgang was resting, a number of other passengers sat down on the empty seat next to him, but none of them stayed there for long. When he woke up, the train was crowded and a number of people were standing in the corridor, even though the seat next to Wolfgang was still vacant. He pointed to it several times, but all of the standing passengers shook their heads and declined, many of them giving him a look that indicated he must be joking.

'What's wrong with me?' wondered Wolfgang.

Suddenly, he realised that he was smelly! He hadn't had a wash since leaving Gotland and, even then, it had been a quick rinse in a bucket of cold water. In the meantime, he had done a lot of running and sweating, both from exertion and from extreme fear.

'As soon as I've reached my next destination, I'll find somewhere to have a bath,' he decided.

His next destination, a monument in the centre of Budapest, was easy to find. Wolfgang stood beneath its central column, gazing up at the statue of the Archangel Gabriel holding the crown of Saint Stephen, the first king of Hungary, in his hand. Then, he walked around the sides of the building, marvelling at the detailed statues of the warriors and statesmen who had founded the country. He had just completed his tour of inspection when he received the sixth set of coordinates from the wolves:

Having noted them down, Wolfgang strolled round to the back of the monument where he noticed a flat bronze plate set in the ground. The plate marked the spot where an artesian well had been sunk to a depth of 971 metres. The well released a hot-water spring that supplied an astonishing 831 litres a minute, at a steady warm temperature. The water was then pumped to the Szechenyi Baths, a huge palace-like building in the nearby City Park.

'Just the ticket!' chuckled the youngster, hurrying off for his much-needed wash.

Hungarian was not one of the languages with which Wolfgang was familiar, so he had to resort to pointing and smiling in order to buy some soap, a towel and a pair of swimming trunks from a colourful little shop in the Szechenyi Baths foyer.

Then, being unable to understand the signs, he got lost in a maze of stone corridors and found himself, by accident, in a beauty treatment room. There were huge tins of slimy-looking mud lined up beside the treatment table. Wolfgang looked at the tins in confusion ... who would want to cover themselves in mud, no matter how good it was for your skin?

Eventually, the smell of chlorine led Wolfgang to the swimming pool. It was a powerful and evocative smell that immediately triggered another flashback to his childhood. He remembered being about ten years old and going swimming with his best friend. It was the first time they had been allowed to go to the swimming pool on their own and the sense of freedom and excitement this created came flooding back into his mind. He vividly recalled being told not to run by the poolside attendant, but hardly being able to stop himself as he saw the water.

Back in the present, Wolfgang felt the same juvenile urgency and hurried as he entered the big, uncrowded changing rooms.

The showers were scalding hot and the teenager gave himself a good wash before making his way into one of the pools. This particular pool was housed in a vast chamber that made the shouts and splashes of the swimmers echo across the room. Wolfgang was not a particularly good swimmer, so he did not venture into the deep end. Instead, he lolled about in the shallows, enjoying the luxurious feel of the warm, clear water swirling around his body. Then, he spotted the chess! Like an ancient Roman spa, people spent all day in these baths and a row of chess tables had been set up for the visitors' recreation. One line of players sat on the edge of the pool, facing the tables. Their opponents stood knee-deep in the water on the other side.

Wolfgang loved chess; it was his favourite game. So, he waited until a space became vacant on the side of the pool and sat down, waiting to play anyone who chose to take him on. It was not long before he had a number of competitors who wished to play him. He had quite a struggle against an older Hungarian man, but eventually triumphed, and wiped the floor with a Swiss girl and a middle-aged German man, much to their annoyance. Wolfgang was staring down, concentrating on putting the pieces back in position, when his next opponent sat down at his table.

'Ready for a lesson in chess?' asked a cold Swedish voice. Looking up, Wolfgang felt the colour instantly drain from his face. Standing opposite him, in a dull, brown swimming costume, was Petra!

Wolfgang's first instinct was to run, but Petra grabbed hold of his right arm and held it in a vice-like grip.

'Stay for your lesson, Wolfgang,' she ordered, picking up the king, the queen, and the knight in her free hand. 'These pieces represent my husband, myself and my son,' she sneered, lining up the pieces on the board. 'This worthless piece of junk is YOU!' she said, picking up a pawn. 'You're just a pawn in OUR game!' Then, she threw the king and the knight into the swimming pool. 'Thanks to you,' she hissed, 'the king is missing and the knight is in hospital, badly injured. Now, that just leaves the queen and the pawn. I think you'll find that the queen's going to take the pawn – and there's nothing you can do about it!'

Just then, two boisterous children rushed past, chasing each other through the shallows. They splashed Petra, startling her and causing her to loosen her grip. That was all Wolfgang needed. Pushing the table forwards, he knocked Petra into the water and scrambled back to the comparative safety of the men's changing rooms. Barely bothering to dry himself, he changed hurriedly and made for the exit. But, Perta was waiting for him outside the changing room door, wearing a multi-coloured bath robe and some flip-flops. She grabbed him painfully by the ear and told him, in no uncertain terms, that he would be in for much more pain if he did not come quietly.

Wolfgang had never struck a woman before, but

these were exceptional circumstances. His quest, indeed the whole future of humankind, depended on his staying free. So, Wolfgang jabbed his elbow sharply into Petra's stomach and raced away as she doubled up, gasping. However, the incident had been witnessed by a security official, who charged after Wolfgang, thinking him to be the one in the wrong. Petra stood and watched with a gleeful, cold-hearted smile. Her job was being done for her now.

Fleeing down the wide corridors of the stately building, Wolfgang knew that he would not get away by speed alone. The guard was gaining on him with every stride and it was only a matter of time before he'd get caught. Then, he found himself approaching the treatment room that he had entered earlier by mistake and a cunning idea flashed into his mind. Wolfgang nipped inside and snatched one of the large tins of mud. Then, tipping it all over the floor just around a corner, he let himself be seen by the guard and disappeared, causing the man to charge after him. Rounding the corner, the security guard skidded on the mud and his legs went right up in the air before he hit the ground with a painful thump.

Petra heard the commotion and rushed to see if Wolfgang had finally been caught. Then, like an action replay from a comedy out-take show, she rounded the corner and slid on the mud also, landing on top of the irate security guard. Covered from head to toe in the slimy mud, and struggling to get to her feet, Petra let out a chilling cry of anger and frustration.

Wolfgang grinned at the scene from the exit, about to make his escape.

'Checkmate!' he said.

Chapter 6

Enter the Gladiatrix

Boarding the plane to Rome, Wolfgang felt incredibly nervous. He had toyed with the idea of continuing his quest on the train, but it was a much longer journey, so he decided to bite the bullet and fly. Time was of the essence. Wolfgang estimated that each chosen young person only had six or seven weeks to search their respective continents and find their Astral Legacy. He knew, that any delay on his part would reduce the amount of time left for the remaining children. After the trials and tribulations that he had suffered trying to retrieve the European Legacy, Wolfgang knew that extra time could make the difference between success and failure. Failure was not an option!

Purchasing the airline ticket had awakened a memory of the plane crash from which he was the sole survivor. He tried to put the fact that he'd experienced the terrors of a fatal airline disaster right out of his mind and tell himself that air travel was, statistically, the safest mode of transport.

As the plane thundered down the runway and soared into the air, Wolfgang tried to distract himself and work out how Petra had located his whereabouts. He presumed that Helmar must have contacted her from his hospital bed in Vienna, and that she had flown down to continue the chase. It terrified Wolfgang that this cold-hearted woman was now on his tail and could easily put a stop to his apocalyptic quest. Plus, the mystery still remained as to how, like her son, she seemed to know exactly where to find him. At least she was not on the flight. He had carefully scrutinised all of the passengers before committing himself to getting on board.

As the plane levelled out at high altitude, Wolfgang closed his eyes and tried to get some much-needed sleep, but a bald-headed man with round glasses, sitting in the seat next to him, insisted on chatting. The man introduced himself as Dr. Henry Walsh, an international expert on wolves, who was going to Rome to study an urban pack that had built a den in the suburbs. Wolfgang listened in silence as the man bored him rigid with a lot of information about wolves that was quite incorrect, or based soley on the behaviour of wolves in captivity. Wolfgang longed to put this pompous stranger right about many things, but he held his tongue.

'May I say,' said Dr. Walsh, patting his young companion on the arm, as they began their descent to Leonardo da Vinci International Airport, 'you look a bit like a wolf yourself.'

'Really?' exclaimed Wolfgang. 'Nobody's ever noticed that before!'

Wolfgang's destination was one of the most famous landmarks in Rome, a building with a long and bloody history. Reading the guidebook that he bought with his admission ticket, Wolfgang was struck by the similarity between his own situation and that of the famous gladiators, who fought and died in this arena. They had no choice but to fight for their lives and hope against hope that they would survive. He felt much the same – only he had the added responsibility of fighting for the lives of every single living person on the planet as well! He was still pondering this curious historical parallel when the wolves made telepathic contact with him once again. With a careful hand, he noted down the coordinates of his next destination at the back of his now dog-eared puzzle book:

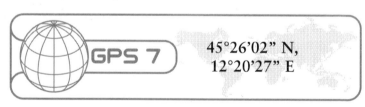

GPS 7

45°26'02" N,
12°20'27" E

Looking up, Wolfgang half expected to see Petra's menacing figure striding towards him, but there was no sign of his enemy this afternoon. So, he decided to take a little time out and look around the amphitheatre. The giant walls of the circular stone building had only fallen down in places, a real miracle considering the numerous earthquakes and wars of the past two thousand years and a testament to the brilliance of Roman engineering. The tiers of banked stone seats, capable of seating 50,000 people, were more-or-less intact and it was easy to imagine the huge crowd, driven wild by bloodlust, cheering for their favourite gladiator or begging the emperor for him to be spared. Most striking of all, Wolfgang was surprised to find that the ancient arena had no floor. Instead, there was just a maze of underground stone walls with a modern walkway built across the top. The walls had once divided different areas under the floor into rooms, where the gladiators and the animals had waited before making their appearance in the arena. Wolfgang decided to go and explore this underground level. He hoped that it would enable him to better understand what it must have felt like to take part in a gladiatorial contest.

It proved to be cold, gloomy and very depressing walking through these ancient passageways.

Wolfgang was longing to return to the brightness of the spring sunshine when he heard an all-too-familiar voice on the nearby steps, questioning one of the tour guides in very bad Italian.

'Sure you haven't seen him?' asked Petra, insistently. 'A gaunt-looking teenager in a denim jacket. Face like a wolf. I know he's in here somewhere!'

Wolfgang shrank back into the shadows. He hoped that if he stayed down where it was dark, she wouldn't find him.

Holding up her iPhone to receive the maximum signal, Petra located Wolfgang's whereabouts, and descended the flight of stone steps into the maze of corridors below. By now, it was late afternoon and the other visitors were leaving in droves, eager to get back to their hotels for a refreshing shower before dinner. Consequently, Petra and Wolfgang soon found themselves alone in the remains of the underground rooms, commissioned by the Emperor Vespasian around 75 AD.

'Come out, come out, wherever you are!' called Petra, demonically. 'You'll make life much easier for everyone if you come quietly. Why don't you give yourself up?'

Wolfgang was tempted to shout 'Never!' but he knew that would give his position away. Instead, he crouched motionless in a dank corner, where water dripped steadily down the slimy green walls, waiting for Petra to pass.

Wolfgang's plan might have worked had it not been for a long cobweb, thick with dust and draped across the corridor like a miniature tennis net, that tickled his nose and made him sneeze. Although he managed to stifle the noise, it was enough to alert Petra to his whereabouts.

'Got you!' she snarled, charging in and trying to grab him by the hair. Wolfgang ducked under her grasp and ran off down one of the crumbling stone corridors. Petra pounded after him, furious that she had come so close but had been thwarted again. So, a deadly game of cat-and-mouse began, which was played out as the sun began to set over Rome.

The chase ended in the strangest of fashions. Petra appeared to suddenly lose patience and give up, stomping back up the stone steps with a loud sigh of resignation. Had she really thrown in the towel, or was it just a trick to lure him out? Either way, Wolfgang did not fancy spending the night in this bleak and spooky place, so he waited until it grew dark before venturing up the steps and attempting to tiptoe away.

The moon was concealed behind a cloud, so Wolfgang stepped onto the modern walkway in total darkness. Suddenly, as the moon emerged and illuminated the walkway, Wolfgang could see the unmistakable silhouette of a gladiator blocking his exit. Like a retiarius or net-fighting gladiator, Petra had armed herself with a long, pronged stick, like a trident, and had several large stones piled up by her feet. She was also holding some heavy-duty netting that she'd discovered beside some workmens' tools nearby. Petra looked a terrifying adversary, but Wolfgang knew that he would have to get past her if he wanted to complete the aliens' life or death test.

Dodging the stones, which Petra furiously pelted at him, Wolfgang charged at her with a wolf-like howl, attempting to barge her off the walkway. It was a bad strategy, as his crouching form made him an easy target for the net. Spreading it out with a graceful sweep of her arm, Petra covered Wolfgang, who immediately tripped over, tangling himself in the knotted strands.

'Now, are you going to walk out of here,' she sniped, triumphantly yanking him to his feet, 'or do I have to drag you all the way back to Sweden?'

The wolves were waiting outside the front entrance to the ancient building. They had heard Wolfgang's howl and had made their way through the backstreets and alleyways, all with the same intention – to rescue their special wolf-brother!

Before Petra even realised what was going on, a powerful she-wolf, with a white-tipped tail, leapt forward and pinned her to the ground. Meanwhile, four young male wolves began tearing at the net with their sharp teeth. Soon, they had made a hole big enough for Wolfgang to wriggle through.

Waiting for their human kinsman to safely disappear into the distance, the wolves melted back into the night, leaving a defeated Petra lying motionless on the pavement.

Chapter 7

The City of Water

Early the next morning, sitting on the first train of the day to Venice, Wolfgang tried to recall if Petra had a weakness that he could exploit. He was sure that she had only been delayed by the Roman wolves and would doubtless come after him again. But, try as he might, he could not think of anything that made her vulnerable. Although she was thin, she was tough, physically fit and possessed an iron will. These traits, combined with an almost complete lack of emotion, made her a formidable adversary.

It was a five-hour journey north and Wolfgang was excited by the prospect of seeing the picturesque Italian countryside, and the beautiful cities of Florence and Padua through which they would pass. Unfortunately, his desire to see any historical sites were dashed when it started to rain.

He hoped it would just be a spring shower, but the rain clouds became increasingly heavy and black, bringing torrential rain that looked set in for the day. Seeing nothing but grey mist and spray out of the train window, Wolfgang sat back in his seat and took the satnav unit out of his backpack. Double-checking his special destination in Venice, Wolfgang prayed that his relentless pursuer wouldn't also be there.

Venice has been called 'The City of Bridges,' 'The City of Water,' 'The City of Light' and 'The Queen of the Adriatic'. Of these, 'The City of Water' seemed the most appropriate as Wolfgang emerged from St Lucia Station to be greeted by a vengeful, Venetian sky. The city was swept by rain. It ran down the colourful facades of the beautiful old buildings and hissed into the network of canals that criss-crossed the city. Wolfgang watched piteously as a young couple passed him by in an open-top gondola. Observing how wet, and cold, they were getting in this traditional mode of Venetian transport, Wolfgang opted to take a modern water-bus, called a vaporetti, to his next destination. The vaporetti chugged around the main canals, picking people up and setting them down, just like a road bus. The stop nearest to his destination was St Mark's Square, the wide stone piazza considered to be the heart of Venice.

The moment he came ashore, Wolfgang experienced another vivid flashback to his previous life. The tall tower in the background, the buildings on either side, with their regular semi-circular archways, and the throng of people hurrying in all directions, reminded him of being a young child and sitting on his late father's knee, staring at a painting on the wall opposite. The picture was of St Mark's Square and was painted by Canaletto. At the time, Wolfgang could not believe that someone had painted this detailed scene – it looked too real.

The flashback rapidly disappeared as he stepped into the square and water gushed over the tops of his trainers. He was standing at the lowest point in

Venice and it was very prone to flooding during heavy rain. Already, the drains were starting to overflow. As he walked through the driving rain, Wolfgang glimpsed a fast-moving, black shape darting beneath one of the dislodged drain covers, but he paid no attention to it. It was probably just a pigeon, for which St Mark's Square was famous.

On the way to his next location, Wolfgang purchased a guidebook and read that the structure he was seeking crossed a narrow canal and connected the Doge's Palace with an ancient prison in the building opposite. The Doge was the ruler of medieval Venice and was a rich and powerful figure. He had maintained his wealth and status by imprisoning his opponents and rivals. It was Lord Byron, the infamous English poet, who gave this enclosed, white limestone bridge its unusual name. Wolfgang imagined the Doge's prisoners sighing loudly, as they caught their last sight of the beautiful city before being taken down to their cells.

Wolfgang was inside the bridge, looking through the stone bars across to the canal below, when the wolves contacted him with the coordinates for the next leg of his journey:

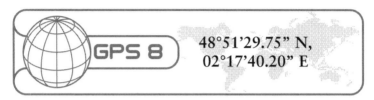

GPS 8   48°51'29.75" N,
02°17'40.20" E

The sense of achievement as Wolfgang noted down this latest set of coordinates was short-lived. As he was busy putting away his notebook and pen, he happened to glance down and saw his arch-enemy, Petra, passing beneath the bridge. She was standing in the back of a water taxi, and was looking through a pair of binoculars.

Making his way back into the Doge's Palace, Wolfgang considered hiding out in its fusty interior for the rest of the day. A stern-faced security guard put paid to that idea when he announced that the building was to close, due to essential flood maintenance work. Preoccupied by the reappearance of Petra, Wolfgang hurried out of the building and into the square, where the rain was falling like liquid curtains.

One enterprising street-seller was braving the elements, offering plastic jackets and waterproof coats to the city's many visitors. Wolfgang chose a hooded top that would not only keep him dry, but also hide a good deal of his face and help to disguise him. Feeling more confident that he would not be spotted, the youngster hurried into a crowded café and, over a pepperoni pizza and a frothy Italian coffee, used his satnav system to find out where he had to go next. The new destination was many miles away, which meant that Wolfgang would need to catch a flight from Venice's Marco Polo International Airport.

Petra was waiting for Wolfgang as he came out of the café. He took one look at her glowering face and shot off, splashing his way through the flood water that was now ankle-deep. He had no idea where he was going, he just wanted to put some distance between himself and Petra. Just as he reached the front of St Mark's Basilica, the Venetian Cathedral, a guided tour party gathered to look at the bronze horse statues outside. Wolfgang joined them, slotting into the shuffling melee and trying to lose himself in the crowd. He thought that he had succeeded until he felt something cold against his wrist. At first, Wolfgang thought he'd become a pickpocket victim. Then, a gentle, well-oiled clicking noise made him realise that it was much more serious than that. Petra was standing next to him – and she had handcuffed him!

Never in his short, but highly eventful life had Wolfgang felt such despair. He was a prisoner again and his quest was over. He had failed! He had let down his loyal wolf-kin and condemned the rest of humanity to oblivion in a few months' time.

Wolfgang wanted to scream and throw himself to the ground, but he could not even vent his frustrations as he was shackled to Petra who held a knife to his side. Forced to hold her hand and smile, the two enemies gave onlookers the impression that they were a loving mother and son.

Wolfgang saw the first rat clearly as they splashed back towards Petra's waiting water taxi. The fat, black rodent scurried from one overflowing drain to another, diving down amidst a chorus of squealing that revealed the presence of many more rats beneath. The sight made Wolfgang feel wildly excited. Of course! That was it! Rats were Petra's weakness! When several rats had been caught in his stone attic prison in Gotland, Petra had fled hysterically from the scene, sobbing that she had to live in a place that was infested with vermin.

They had almost reached the water taxi, so Wolfgang had to act quickly. Spotting a small, dark inlet with more wriggling shapes at the end of it, the desperate teenager suddenly yanked his captor down the slippery footpath and pointed to the seething rats, that were now cornered by their arrival. Petra dropped the knife and was immediately paralysed with fear.

'Let me go and I won't make you go any closer,' hissed Wolfgang.

'You'll pay for this!' blustered Petra.

Wolfgang's response was to jerk her several paces forwards, so the rats started running over her feet.

'All right, all right!' she screamed, fumbling frantically with the key to release the handcuffs. The moment he was released, Wolfgang fled and expected Petra to follow. But, she just stood there, rooted with terror. The cornered rats went on the offensive, squealing loudly and leaping at her from all directions. One clung to her arm, another crawled up her leg, and a third landed on her hair, before scurrying down the back of her neck. With a shrill scream that echoed around the ancient walls, she maniacally fled up the path. Due to the deluge of rain, the pavement was very slippery and Petra promptly lost her footing, falling into the black, stagnant water below. The last view that Wolfgang saw, before he fled towards the airport, was of Petra floating face down in the canal, while a tourist dialled urgently on her mobile phone for emergency assistance.

Chapter 8

An Up and Down Day

Much to his annoyance, Wolfgang's flight to Paris was delayed by nine hours due to the torrential rain. Large pools of water had gathered on the runways, making it too dangerous to operate the planes. The excessive rainfall of the past two days had caused a great deal of damage in Northern Europe and now the weather system had moved further south. It meant that the restless teenager had no choice but to sit impatiently at the airport, watching crowds of people building up in the lounges and restaurants, like water behind a dam.

Amidst the busy scene, Wolfgang thought his mind was playing tricks on him when he caught a glimpse of someone who looked exactly like Nils Ohlson, pushing his way through the queues downstairs. He quickly dismissed this sighting, assured that the greedy scientist was still a prisoner of the wolves, and was doubtless eating berries and grubs in the dark forests of Gotland at that very moment.

It was mid-evening by the time Wolfgang's flight finally touched down at Charles de Gaulle International Airport, making it difficult for him to decide whether to go straight to his destination or wait until the next morning. He chose to wait, and as a cold, damp wind was blowing through Paris, Wolfgang began his search for a cheap hotel.

Although he'd cleaned out all of Nils's bank accounts and made some profit on the sale of the convertible, money was rapidly dwindling away. Wolfgang calculated that he still had enough to complete his quest, but he would have to be very frugal from now on. That meant a hotel near the airport, or one in the centre of Paris, was completely out of the question. He was forced to take the Metro underground railway to the outskirts of the city, eventually finding a rundown boarding house near the Gare du Nord Railway Station.

It was a dull room at the top of the building and although basic, the bed was clean and comfortable, allowing the weary traveller the best night's sleep he'd had in ages.

The next morning, Wolfgang was up bright and early, looking forward to getting on with his quest. Gulping down a bowl-sized cup of hot chocolate, into which he dipped some freshly-baked bread rolls, he paid his moderate bill and headed back towards the Metro. Wolfgang had to wait to cross the road while a Parisian street-cleaning machine went by, beeping loudly as it sprayed powerful jets of water into the gutters.

'That would make a great water pistol,' thought the teenager, with a chuckle.

Wolfgang arrived at the Champ de Mars, the site of Paris's greatest tourist attraction and the most-visited monument in the world, just before it opened. As he waited, he kicked his foot impatiently against one of the gigantic iron pillars.

'Mind you don't knock it down, Wolfgang,' said

Nils, stepping out of the shadows.

'So it was you!' gasped the youngster, feeling dismay grip the inside of his stomach like a hand. 'How on earth ...?'

'So, you can talk as well as drive,' spat Nils. 'Anyway, I got lucky,' continued the bearded Swede, smugly. 'The rainstorms caused a landslide that swept away my two flea-ridden wolf guards. Seizing the chance, I got out of the forest, bought myself a new passport, received a little text from my darling wife and here I am ...'

Nils found himself uttering the end of his sentence into thin air. Wolfgang had vanished!

Hiding in the darkness behind one of the pillars, Wolfgang watched Nils hurrying off in the opposite direction, muttering furiously under his breath. Seeking cover, he swiftly joined a passing party of Spanish secondary school children who were not in school uniform and blended in perfectly. He queued up with them to pay his entrance fee to the national monument, but parted company as they took the lift to the first level. Wolfgang did not want to find himself trapped in such a confined space, electing to climb the 328 steps instead. With throbbing legs and a pounding head, he neared the first floor lobby – only to spot that his furious pursuer was already there! Taking evasive action, Wolfgang charged back down to the ground floor, jarring his knees with every step.

'Come on, Lupe,' he gasped out loud. 'When are you going to get in touch? I need to get away from this place!'

It was now clear that Wolfgang was required to reach the uppermost observation platform before he would be given the next set of coordinates. The lifts were getting crowded with visitors, so he took a chance and pressed himself into a corner, shielded by a wide American couple, and managed to reach the top without being spotted. He would have liked to have spent some time admiring the panoramic views over the French capital, picking out famous landmarks like the Arc de Triomphe, the avenue

Champs-Elysées, and Notre Dame Cathedral, but there was no time. The tingling sensation commenced immediately and he hurriedly noted down the vital coordinates as they flashed into his brain:

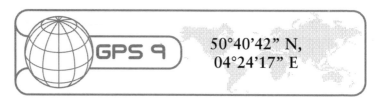

GPS 9

50°40'42" N,
04°24'17" E

Flushed with success, Wolfgang took a final look around and started to make his way down again, only to discover Nils waiting on the second floor lobby, looking left and right like someone watching a tennis match at Wimbledon. Timing his run perfectly, Wolfgang dodged into the Jules Verne Restaurant without being spotted by his pursuer.

The prices in the restaurant took Wolfgang's breath away. He was about to leave when he was set upon by the formidable head waiter, who insisted that he should order something. Not wishing to make a scene, and attract the attention of

Nils, Wolfgang spent a small fortune on a minuscule cup of coffee and a croque-monsieur, a tasty, grilled ham and cheese sandwich that was gone in a couple of bites. Wolfgang may as well have saved his money, because just as he was about to leave, his former captor sat down in the empty seat opposite, exposing a stun gun that was concealed beneath his raincoat.

'You've had your fun, Wolf Boy,' he growled. 'My wife and son are both in hospital, thanks to you. I've no intention of ending up the same way, so how about you and I become friends? I'll make it worth your while. Cooperate with me and I'll cut you 30 per cent of the profits.'

'Get lost!' shouted Wolfgang, as he pulled the tablecloth, causing an avalanche of cutlery and crockery to crash onto the hard stone floor. The resulting chaos created a scene that delayed Nils and gave Wolfgang the chance to escape.

By now, there was a massive queue for the lift, so Wolfgang took to the stairs once again. With aching limbs, he thundered down the 340 steps to the first floor and the further 328 to the ground floor. Nils soon came after him, threatening him with the stun gun and gaining on him with every second. Reaching the bottom at last, Wolfgang's knees throbbed and his limbs felt like jelly – he knew he could not run much further.

Losing Nils in the heaving crowds, Wolfgang noticed a small workmens' café across the road from the Champ de Mars, where the Parisian street cleaners met for lunch. Wolfgang realised, with sudden excitement, that the latest arrival had just jumped out of his water-cart and hurried inside, leaving his keys in the ignition. An idea flashed into Wolfgang's racing brain. Ignoring the angry hoots from passing cars, he skipped across the road and jumped into the cart. Rapidly familiarising himself with the controls, Wolfgang started the engine and swung the little vehicle around, just as Nils spotted him and crossed the road. SCOOOSH! Wolfgang activated the street-washing nozzles, aiming a high velocity jet of water directly at his enemy. SCOOOSH! It went straight into Nils's eyes and mouth, temporarily blinding and choking him, before knocking him backwards into the gutter. Defeated, Nils slunk away, soaking wet and spluttering, leaving a trail of wet footprints behind him.

Chapter 9

The Nearest-Run Thing You Ever Saw in Your Life

Sitting on a smart, high-speed train to Brussels, Wolfgang wrestled with the baffling problem of how his pursuers always seemed to know his exact location. First Helmar, then Petra, and now Nils himself were always there right behind him, no matter where he went. It irritated him enormously that he could not work out their secret. With a resigned shrug of his shoulders, he took the satnav system out of his rucksack to double-check the details of his next destination in Belgium.

In his previous life, Wolfgang's passion for history had focused predominantly on the eighteenth and nineteenth centuries, a time when the modern industrial world was just coming into being. So, he felt very excited at the prospect of heading for a famous historic site, the battlefield of

Waterloo where The Duke of Wellington had finally defeated Napoleon, on June 18th, 1815.

The thought of this visit triggered a powerful flashback to an incident at Wolfgang's school, about a year before he boarded the ill-fated flight. He had been talking in class instead of listening to his uninspiring history teacher. Suddenly, the teacher had stopped talking and invited Wolfgang out to the front of the class, determined to embarrass the boy.

'If you know so much that you can afford to talk when I'm talking,' he chided, 'then why don't you take the lesson instead of me?'

'Very well, sir,' replied Wolfgang. 'If you insist ...'

He proceeded to relate the story of the Battle of Waterloo in gripping detail, brilliantly illustrating Wellington's assertion that it had been 'the nearest-run thing you ever saw in your life'. His classmates were enthralled by the vivid account, listening in absolute silence and applauding him at the end. When the bell rang for the end of the lesson, the humiliated teacher walked out in disgust, much to the amusement of Wolfgang's classmates. As this pleasant flashback faded, he tried his hardest to remember his name at school, but it eluded him.

The countryside grew increasingly flat and uninteresting as the train sped through Belgium, pulling into Brussels station just after midday.

Wolfgang fancied taking a look at the European Parliament, but, as usual, the urgency of his mission forced him onwards.

He caught a bus that took him south of the city, to the town of Waterloo. It was a surprisingly busy place with two massive supermarkets, a posh hotel, banks and offices and two big international schools. There were also rows of shops selling souvenirs of the great battle that had made the town famous. It saddened Wolfgang to think that even today, nearly two hundred years after the event, people were making money from the 50,000 or so soldiers who were either killed or wounded on that blood-soaked Sunday afternoon.

There was no doubting Wolfgang's next location,

about a mile away from the town; it was a huge mound with a gigantic animal statue on the top. The monument was ordered by King William I of the Netherlands and was built between 1820–1826, to mark the spot where his son, the Prince of Orange, had been hit in the shoulder by a musket ball during the battle. The Prince, who later became King William II, was seen as a national hero by the Belgians, despite the fact that his leadership during the conflict had been hopeless.

Paying his six euros for admission, Wolfgang climbed the 226 steps to the observation platform at the top, his stiff knees starting to throb once again. But, it was worth it. The view over the battlefield was magnificent and, once he was standing beside the statue, the wolves gave him the GPS coordinates of his final destination:

GPS 10

51°30'03.40" N
0°08'31.20" W

With these all-important figures safely recorded in his puzzle book, Wolfgang relaxed a little and stood looking out over the silent, grassy fields, where once there had been screaming, gunfire and mayhem.

Meanwhile, in the car park below, Nils was just arriving in a police car with two Belgian officers. One was a slow-speaking sergeant called Verbeke and the other was a stocky constable called Smets, who was bereft of any sense of humour or fun.

'There he is!' exclaimed the Swede, pointing excitedly at the top of the monument. 'What are you waiting for? Go and arrest him!'

'Hang on a minute, sir,' drawled Sergeant Verbeke, not taking kindly to being told what to do. 'Let's get your story straight first. You claim that the young man up there is your adopted son, you say he stole your money to finance a sightseeing trip around Europe, and now you want him back so he can work for you and pay back all of the money he's spent?'

'That's it in a nutshell!' snapped Nils, becoming concerned that Wolfgang would spot him and get away again.

'Very well, then,' agreed Verbeke, after a long pause. 'Let's interview this son of yours and hear his side of the story.'

Having to climb the steps to the top of the monument did nothing to improve Constable Smets's humour. The portly officer had to pause every fifty steps or so to get his breath back and, to Nils watching from below, it seemed to take him forever to reach the top. Wolfgang was still lost in the panoramic view of the battlefield when he felt the firm tap on his shoulder. Turning around, he was shocked to find that he was face to face with a policeman. More alarmingly, he observed that a second officer was waiting with Nils at the base of the mound. Panicking, Wolfgang hooked his left foot behind Smets's calves and pushed him backwards, sending the startled constable sprawling to the ground. Then, with a gymnastic-like spring,

Wolfgang vaulted the railing and started running down the steep hill with the police officer in hot pursuit. Waving his arms up and down like a high-wire artist, Wolfgang managed to keep his footing, but the burly policeman was not so fortunate. He lost his balance on the steepest part of the hill and tumbled over a number of times, before sprawling to a painful stop in a hollow. By the time he was on his feet again, Wolfgang had reached the bottom of the hill and was looking for somewhere to hide.

Wolfgang's flight convinced Sergeant Verbeke of his guilt, so the policeman decided to grant Nils's wish and arrest the boy on suspicion of theft. It should have been easy to apprehend the runaway, as there were only a handful of shops, bars and museums at the foot of the monument. But, as always, Wolfgang proved to be cunning and elusive. He dodged Smets in the Waterloo Museum, leading the fuming constable a merry dance around the exhibits before slipping out of the emergency exit. Nils nearly caught his 'adopted son' hiding in the toilets of one of the bars, but Wolfgang escaped through a window. Then, Verbeke cornered him in a souvenir shop, only to be thwarted when Wolfgang pushed a display stand over on top of him, much to the horror of the outraged shopkeeper. It could only be a matter of time before one of them caught the fugitive ... but then, he completely disappeared!

The trio searched everywhere, becoming angrier and more bewildered with every passing minute. Where had he gone? He seemed to have disappeared into thin air!

Meanwhile, a young tour guide wearing an ill-fitting blue jacket, and an official peaked cap pulled down right over his eyes, tiptoed out of the little white tourist office, gently closing the door so as not to wake the elderly tour guide, who was sleeping peacefully in his chair. The young official met a coach load of tourists who had come to visit the battlefield, delighting them with his gripping description of the famous battle, which he delivered to the multinational party in fluent English, French and German.

At the end of the tour, the grateful vistors gathered around their talented guide, showering him with thanks and pressing generous tips into his hand. At the same time, two miserable-looking Belgian policemen and a furious-looking Swedish man marched back to their car and set off for Brussels to file a report on a completely unsuccessful day. Wolfgang watched the police car until it disappeared into the distance.

'That was the second nearest-run thing you ever saw in your life!' he said to himself.

Chapter 10

Pussycat, Pussycat, Where Have You Been?

Eager to complete the final stage of his mission as quickly as possible, Wolfgang enquired about flights to England, only to discover that last-minute bookings were very expensive and beyond his depleted funds. The same was true of the train service to London, so he had no other option but to travel by coach. Pulling out of Brussels bus station, the long, dome-fronted vehicle was immediately caught in heavy traffic and Wolfgang resigned himself to a tedious journey beset by hold-ups and delays. The only good thing about this method of transport was that the same coach went all the way to Victoria coach station in the heart of London, near to his next destination, so he only had to sit tight and he would get there ... eventually!

The ferry was waiting at Ostend to take

Wolfgang and his fellow passengers across to England. It was an enormous white boat, with a red funnel and a cavernous hold that looked like a yawning sea monster. Wolfgang marvelled at the dockworkers' skill as they manoeuvred all of the cars, heavy lorries and coaches to within a few inches of each other without causing a crash.

Climbing the narrow staircases to the main deck, Wolfgang settled back in a comfortable seat beside a porthole and began flicking through a magazine that had been left on the seat beside him. It was a motoring magazine and the teenager noticed, with keen interest, that the satnav system he had taken from Nils's convertible was reviewed and rated as one of the best. The key features of the satnav were listed under a picture of the device and what Wolfgang read next made him sit bolt-upright with shock.

'Recommended for its anti-theft tracking system, the main unit emits a powerful signal that can be tracked on any computer, or even on your iPhone.'

So that was it! His pursuers had received constant updates of his whereabouts from the satnav that he was using to complete the quest. At last, the mystery of how he had been followed was solved!

Having already discovered his final location, Wolfgang no longer needed the system. So, flinging the magazine aside he marched out on deck, leaned over the side and dropped it into the murky waters of the harbour.

'Good riddance!' he exclaimed, watching the device disappear with a gurgle of bubbles. Returning to his comfy seat, he felt safe in the knowledge that Nils could no longer find out where he was. As Wolfgang began to relax, little did he know that a last-minute passenger had joined the ship just before it sailed. Wearing a new suit and sporting a clean-shaven face, a disguised Nils had tracked Wolfgang to the boat prior to the satnav being discarded. Determined to learn from his previous mistakes, Nils had decided to wait patiently and only strike when the time was right, making absolutely sure that his quarry did not escape this time.

The crossing from Ostend to Dover was smooth and enjoyable; the recent storms having abated. Standing on deck, Wolfgang felt another flashback lighting up his memory, as he watched the ferries and container ships making their way in and out of Dover Harbour. He recalled being very young and watching big ships entering and leaving a different harbour. It had been very exciting, sitting on his grandad's shoulders and pointing at all of the different boats, noting their colours and learning their names. Southampton was the place, he suddenly remembered. In his former life, Wolfgang had lived somewhere near the port of Southampton, in England!

The ferry docked at half past nine that evening and it was past eleven o'clock before the weary passengers negotiated Customs and Immigration. After changing what little money he had left from

euros to pounds, Wolfgang climbed back onto the
coach for the last leg of his journey to London. The
timing suited Wolfgang well. He could sleep on the
bus and be ready to resume his quest bright and
early the next morning.

He'd had a nasty moment at Immigration when a
stern-faced woman had looked at his passport for
an unusually long time. Fortunately, she had been
called away to help investigate another passenger,
whose bearded passport photograph looked nothing
like his current appearance. This same passenger
subsequently bought a ticket for Wolfgang's coach,
quietly making his way past a sleeping Wolfgang
and down the aisle to a seat at the back.

The coach should have arrived at the depot in the
small hours of the morning, but there was a long
hold-up on the M25, the congested orbital
motorway that surrounds London, and it did not
actually pull in until just after seven o'clock.
Already, the streets of the capital were thronged
with commuters making their way to work, looking

as grey as the buildings surrounding them.

Stiff, aching and feeling a bit sick, Wolfgang
wandered across to Victoria Railway Station and
paid to use the downstairs cloakrooms, giving
himself a bracing cold water wash at one of the
hand basins. Then, he went up the escalator to the
first floor and spent a sizeable chunk of his
remaining money on a full English breakfast.
Fortified by a stomach full of eggs, bacon, sausages,
baked beans and fried bread, Wolfgang made his
way, with mounting excitement and lightness of
step, to his last prescribed location.

It was only a short walk to this beautiful
building, one of the must-see sights of London and
possibly the best-known royal residence in the
world. He stood by the Victoria Memorial
sculpture, just across the road from the main gates,
and looked directly at the balcony where the royal
family often appeared. He expected the wolves to
contact him with instructions on how to locate the
European Astral Legacy, but, he was disappointed –

there was silence.

Clearly, this final task was going to be more complicated than he had imagined. Wolfgang had been forced to enter the arena in Rome and go right to the top of the monument in Paris. So, he presumed that he would need to get closer to this final destination.

As he crossed the road towards the magnificent residence, Wolfgang was unaware that a man was following him. His stalker was wearing a Union Jack sun hat and was so intent on his business that he forgot to look left or right and nearly went under a red double-decker bus.

A ceremony called the 'Changing of the Guard' was about to take place in the grounds, so Wolfgang joined the ever-growing crowd to watch the proceedings and hoped that this would be the trigger for the wolves to make contact. Again, he was disappointed. Trapped by the pressing crowd behind him, he had no option but to stay and watch the soldiers in their bright red uniforms, and tall, bearskin hats, called busbies, shouting at each other and stamping their feet in a very formal manner. To Wolfgang, it seemed ridiculous, but the hordes of foreign tourists lapped it up and applauded as if they'd been watching a London West End musical.

Followed by his silent shadow, Wolfgang walked around the huge building, admiring its perfectly symmetrical columns and the smooth Portland stone that covered its front facade. How was he going to get inside?

It seemed impossible – until he spotted a long queue in front of a notice advertising 'Guided Tours of the State Rooms'. He was in luck! Normally, public access to the royal residence was restricted to the months of August and September, but this year, in an attempt to raise extra revenue, the rooms had been opened during the Easter holidays as well.

Pulse racing, Wolfgang joined the back of the queue and found himself standing behind a little girl with blonde curls and a white, soft toy cat tucked firmly under one arm.

'Hello,' said Wolfgang, unnerved by her intense gaze. 'What's your name?'

'Ruby,' replied the child.

'That's a pretty name,' he commented.

'Yes, it is,' she agreed. 'What's yours?'

'Wolfgang,' answered the teenager, beginning to regret that he'd started a conversation with the inquisitive little girl.

'That's a funny name!' decided Ruby, immediately being told to leave the nice young man alone by her mother. The little girl took absolutely no notice and thrust her soft toy under Wolfgang's nose.

'This is Jingle-Jean,' she explained, violently shaking the cat to make the bell on its collar tinkle feebly. 'I've brought her with me because of the nursery rhyme. It's my favourite. You can sing it with me if you like.'

Ruby did not wait for a reply and commenced singing:

'Pussycat, pussycat, where have you been?

123

I've been to London to visit the Queen.

Pussycat, pussycat, what did you do there?

I frightened a little mouse, under her chair.'

'That was great!' exclaimed Wolfgang, hoping to bring the conversation to an end.

'It was, wasn't it?' declared Ruby, glowing with excitement. 'Let's sing it again!'

Fortunately, the queue started to move forwards at this point and Wolfgang gladly said goodbye to his young admirer. The admission fee used up his last twenty pound note, leaving him with only a handful of coins, but he did not care. He was totally focused on finding the key to the wolves' final message, which would bring his quest to a successful conclusion.

Once inside the building, Wolfgang left his assigned tour guide and sneaked off into one of the ornately decorated drawing rooms, with pictures by Rubens, Rembrant and Canaletto hanging from the walls.

Hurrying through an elaborate doorway,

Wolfgang found himself in the Throne Room, but there was still no response from the wolves. Unsure as to his next move, he blundered on through the lavish apartments and into the State Dining Room. This room showed what a royal banquet looked like, with long rows of tables covered with immaculate tablecloths, glittering glasses, matching sets of plates bearing the royal crest and sparkling silver cutlery, all laid out to perfection. Wolfgang began fantasising about a delicious royal feast, but the realisation that the wolves had still not made contact brought him swiftly back to reality. Nowhere in any of the State Rooms had triggered the vital response. What was going on? What did the wolves want?

In another of the drawing rooms, Wolfgang bumped into Ruby again. The little girl was trailing along behind her mother, looking bored to tears, but her face brightened as she saw her new friend across the room and lifted Jingle-Jean to wave a paw at him. Suddenly, the solution to this latest part of his quest became clear. Remembering Ruby's nursery rhyme, Wolfgang realised that he would have to see the Queen of England in order to receive the final location from the wolves!

The flag had been flying from the rooftops, so Wolfgang knew that Her Majesty was in residence. But, how was he going to get to see her in the flesh? All of the doors to the residential apartments were roped off and marked PRIVATE. It seemed an impossible final task and Wolfgang experienced a moment of panic and despair, thinking he would fall at this last hurdle. But, the sight of a stuffed and mounted wolf's head looking down at him from one of the walls rekindled his resolve.

A few moments later, an opportunity presented itself, when a butler hurried out through one of the private doors, leaving it unlocked. Without a moment's hesitation, Wolfgang nipped inside, not even thinking what he would do or say if he were caught.

Wolfgang found himself in a maze of carpeted

corridors. Peeping around each corner like a cat burglar, he made his way further and further into the royal apartments. He could hear voices coming from a private sitting room and, as he stood outside the door, he could hear the Queen discussing her forthcoming engagements with her private secretary. Wolfgang decided that he couldn't just burst in, so he hid behind a heavy curtain and waited, hoping that Her Majesty would emerge and he could catch a glimpse of her from his hiding place. But, it did not happen. The voices ceased and Wolfgang realised the Queen had left the room by another door. Cursing his luck, he tiptoed out from behind the curtain and, backing down the corridor, he collided with the butler he had seen earlier.

'What the Dickens are you doing here?' asked the man, sharply.

'I was looking for the toilet,' replied Wolfgang, pretending to be in great distress.

'There are plenty of public toilets,' snapped the butler, looking very suspicious. 'How did you get into this private area?'

'I came in through a door,' said Wolfgang, all his wolf-cunning kicking in at this moment of great peril. 'Someone must have left it open.'

The butler paused. He knew he would be in great trouble if he admitted to such a careless mistake and had allowed an intruder into the Queen's private home. So, without saying another word, the man led Wolfgang to the nearest door, pushed him through it and locked it firmly behind him.

Blowing out his cheeks with relief, Wolfgang realised that he'd just had a very narrow escape – but he was still no closer to seeing the Queen. Then, he noticed that the State Rooms were almost deserted and the remaining visitors were all leaving in a hurry.

'What's going on?' he politely asked one of the guides.

'Her Majesty the Queen is about to leave the building in a royal motorcade,' explained the woman in a rather snooty voice. 'If you hurry outside, you'll be able to see her.'

Wolfgang needed no second bidding! Half-walking and half-running, he sped towards the exit to join the crowds thronging the gates in front of the building.

It was at this moment that Nils chose to strike! He had followed Wolfgang all around the exhibition, unable to seize him because of the crowds, but now it was quiet, and he was waiting to pounce just outside the exit. Seeing Wolfgang charging out towards him, the grinning Swede stuck out his foot, sending the unsuspecting youngster sprawling down the steps and onto the pavement below. Startled and dazed, Wolfgang looked up to find Nils dropping down on him like a wrestler, pinning his arms and legs to the ground.

'You've led us all a merry dance, Wolf Boy,' snarled the disgraced scientist. 'But, this is the end of the road!'

'That's what you think!' retorted Wolfgang, spitting hard in Nils's eye and making him recoil backwards. This was enough to allow the teenager to throw his captor off and escape to an empty sentry box where he hid until his enemy stumbled past, swearing furiously in Swedish.

The Queen was just stepping into a shiny black limousine as Wolfgang arrived at the front gates. Her Majesty looked directly at him and gave a little wave, immediately causing a powerful tingle in his hand and making him scrabble for the puzzle book in his rucksack.

'Congratulations! You have shown great courage and have overcome many obstacles in order to visit the ten locations selected by the aliens. Here are your final instructions,' commanded Lupe's telepathic voice. 'Look at the last puzzle in your book. It's a crossword. Solve the clues and write the names of the ten places you've visited into the grid. When it's full, transfer the letters, highlighted in grey, to the solution boxes below. This must be done in order, using the letters at the top first and then working your way down the grid, from left to right. The completed solution boxes will spell out the name of the place where the third Astral Legacy can be found.

'Your wolf kin are proud of you and will be with you in spirit as you attempt to complete the rest of your quest. Remember, the human race is depending on you!'

After that, there was silence and Wolfgang knew that, sadly, he would have no more contact with the wolves.

The motorcade went on and on, the royal car being followed by lots of other vehicles containing officials, security men and police. After putting away his puzzle book, Wolfgang looked up and saw Nils glaring at him from the opposite side of the motorcade. Trembling with impatience, the kidnapper had to wait for the procession to pass, by which time, Wolfgang was on the move. This left Nils with a big problem. Unable to track the discarded satnav, he did not know where Wolfgang was heading. This meant that he would have to keep his prize in sight. Roughly pushing his way through the crowds, Nils just managed to keep on Wolfgang's tail and followed him back to Victoria Station. There, he caught a glimpse of the teenager stopping at the Information Bureau and then making his way towards the underground.

'Excuse me, sir,' he said, sidling over to the man in the bureau. 'That young man you were just talking to is my runaway son. Could you tell me where he's heading?'

'Salisbury Plain,' replied the official casually, reaching out to answer an insistent telephone.

As Wolfgang emerged from Kew Gardens station, having spent the last of his money getting as far out of London as he could, it started to rain again. This time, it was a steady drizzle; the wetness clung to his clothes like pollen. By the time he had walked over Kew Bridge, looking down at the swirling brown-grey water of the River Thames, and reached the motorway, he was wet through. Wolfgang had no option but to try and hitch a lift to the West

Country, but no one wanted to stop. The cars and lorries swished past in steady succession, sending up occasional swathes of muddy water that soaked him even further. He was cold, tired, wet and hungry, and did not know who he was or where he belonged. He had absolutely no money, no friends and no wolf allies to help him ... and the fate of the whole world still rested on his shoulders.

Suddenly, it all became too much for him. He felt overwhelmed. The will to fight seemed to drain out of him and Wolfgang found himself emitting a series of heart-wrenching sobs, before crouching down with his hands covering his head – the image of total and utter despair.

What happens next?

When you have identified the ten key locations that Wolfgang visits on his quest, use the wolves' clues to help you place them into the crossword grid on pages 136–137. If you insert the words of the answers correctly, the location of the third Astral Legacy will be revealed, highlighted in grey. Enter the letters in order, from top to bottom and left to right, into the box below.

Then, log-on to **www.astrallegacies.com** to report the location of the third legacy. If you successfully enter this final landmark into the website, the adventure is complete, and you will be able to read the thrilling climax to *Wolves' Gambit* online.

Read the book ... find the hidden locations ...
solve the puzzle ... save the world!
www.astrallegacies.com

Across

1. Hösök tere – a major
   square in Budapest,
   Hungary. (6,6)
   GPS CODE 5.

7. Gee up, horsey! A
   famous centre for
   classical dressage in
   Vienna, Austria. (7,6,6)
   GPS CODE 4.

9. Butte du Lion – Let out
   a roar as you battle to
   the top of this. (5,5)
   GPS CODE 9.

10. A former city gate in
    Berlin which features
    on a German banknote.
    (11,4) **GPS CODE 2**.

Solution

The third Astral Legacy is
located at:

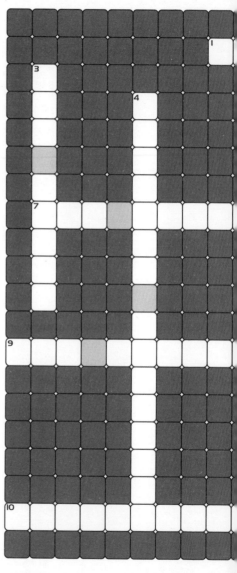

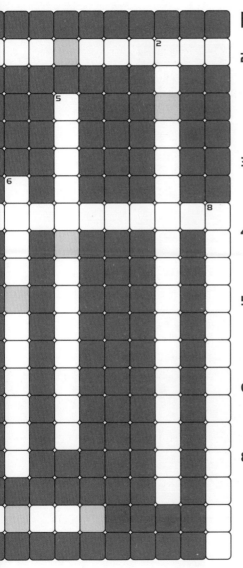

Down

2. A medieval time device, located on the southern wall of the Old Town City Hall in Prague. (12,5) **GPS CODE 3.**

3. World-famous amphitheatre in Rome. (9) **GPS CODE 6.**

4. The grandest royal residence in London. (10,6) **GPS CODE 10.**

5. Ponte dei Sospiri – A 'sad', but famous bridge in Venice. (6,2,5) **GPS CODE 7.**

6. The most famous tower in France. (6,5) **GPS CODE 8.**

8. Something fishy about this small statue, located in Copenhagen harbour, Denmark. (6,7) **GPS CODE 1.**

The Astral Legacies Series

Orcas' Song
The North American Legacy. Book 1

Tigers' Secret
The Asian Legacy. Book 2

The Astral Legacies Series

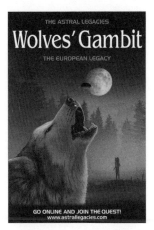

Wolves' Gambit
The European Legacy. Book 3

*Available from
all good
bookshops.*

Notes

Notes

Notes

Notes

About the Author

Gordon Volke's commercial writing career began in 1972 when he was responsible for inventing the comic antics of Dennis the Menace, Minnie the Minx and The Bash Street Kids in the UK's best-selling comic, *The Beano*.

Since this auspicious start to his writing career, Gordon has gained plaudits by originating material for Snoopy (Peanuts), Tom and Jerry, Popeye and Garfield, and has been the principal contributor for numerous comics and magazines, including *Twinkle*, *Thomas the Tank Engine*, *The James Bond Experience* and *Jurassic Park*.

In 1998, Gordon began writing for *The Tweenies*, the Bafta award-winning pre-school series, scripting 44 of the 365 episodes.

Over the years Gordon has originated children's books covering most genres and age categories. He lives near Brighton on the south coast of England.